Anansi
The Trickster Spider

Lynne Garner

ANANSI
THE TRICKSTER SPIDER

"Woe to him who would put his trust in Anansi - a sly, selfish and greedy fellow"

"The wisdom of the spider is greater than that of all the world put together"

(Traditional African proverbs)

To Jon
Thanks for always believing and always supporting

CONTENTS

INTRODUCTION

The antics of Anansi the Trickster Spider (also known as Ananse, Kweku Ananse, Anancy or Aunt Nancy) have been told for centuries by parents and grandparents to children eager to hear of his mischievous ways. It is believed these stories originated in Ghana, Africa and are part of the long oral tradition of the Ashanti people. The word Anansi is a word from the Akan (also known as Twi and Fante) language, which simple means 'spider.' His tales travelled the world with people who migrated and sadly with slaves who were transported to distant lands including the Caribbean and the New World (America).

Now Anansi is as clever as he is lazy, and he loves to prove just how smart he is by tricking the people of the village and the animals of the jungle. Luckily for the people and animals around him Anansi is not always as clever as he likes to think he is. Sometimes things backfire on him and he becomes the victim of his own tricks.

Although I have said Anansi is a spider he also has the power to appear as a man. So sometimes in these stories it is difficult to decide what form he has taken. Is he a spider or is he a man? So, it's been left to you to decide for yourself if you see him with two slightly hairy legs or eight extremely hairy legs.

I hope you enjoy reading them as much as I enjoyed researching and writing them.

Lynne Garner, May 2014.

P.S. If you love art and craft please visit our website www.anansi-spider.com and enjoy the free to download Anansi themed activities.

ANANSI AND THE GUM DOLL

The moon was high in the night sky and the air was cool. Sneaking from his hut, Anansi looked around him. No one else was there to see him creep down to the farmer's field full of just-ripe yams. Quietly, he picked enough yams for his breakfast, his dinner and for his tea the following day. His arms full of yams, he tiptoed back to his hut, climbed into bed, smiled and fell asleep.

The next morning the sun had just climbed out of bed and into the sky and the earth was just beginning to warm under its gentle rays. The farmer in his hut stretched and yawned as he got out of bed. As he stretched his stiff muscles he smiled to himself. "Mmm, just-ripe, fresh yams for breakfast." He couldn't wait. He knew his crop of yams would be ready for picking and he was really looking forward to the breakfast his wife would cook with the yams taken straight from his field at the bottom of the hill. Slipping his shoes and clothes on, he crept out of the house so as not to wake his wife. Outside the sun began to warm his skin; a few of the other villagers had also risen early, so they could make the long walk to market. The farmer also spotted a goat that had escaped its pen and, being in such a good mood, decided he would put it back for his neighbor. Happy with his good deed, he whistled a tune as he strode towards his fields looking forward to the delight of breakfast. With a spring in his step and a tune leaving his lips, he contemplated a day beginning with a full stomach of well cooked yams. For his wife was a brilliant cook and her specialty, yes, you guessed, it was yams!

Whistling loudly as he arrived at the field, he quickly collected a few yams. He sat down on the ground to clean the yams ready to give to his wife to cook. As he collected the prepared yams in his arms he abruptly stopped whistling. To his horror, it looked like some of his prize yams were gone from the field!

"Who could have done such a thing?" Very upset, the farmer ran home. Bursting in through the door, the farmer shouted to his wife, "Someone has taken some of our yams. What am I to do?"

Sure her husband had miscounted the yams, she put her arm around his shoulders. "I'm sure we'll get to the bottom of this, and after a good breakfast of my special yams it won't look so bad," she reassured him.

Soon the missing yams were forgotten as the freshly cooked breakfast passed the farmer's lips and warmed his stomach. Enjoying every mouthful, he decided to recount the yams in his field and then tend his other fields. Once breakfast was over the farmer visited his yams field and counted again. He was sure he was right and that some of his yams were missing. However, perhaps his wife was right and he had miscounted or remembered the wrong number of yams. So this time he wrote the number down, but as he did not have a pencil and paper, using pebbles he wrote the number in the earth, under a tree.

The rest of the day the farmer spent tending his other crops in the next field. Whilst tending his crops he decided to count them all and carefully placed the number in the earth as before. As he did not have a pencil and paper he used pebbles, placing them in the earth by a large rock at the edge of his field.

That night a few clouds drifted across the night sky, but the moon was high and the air was cool. Anansi popped his head out of his hut as he checked the coast was clear. Quietly, he tiptoed down to the field, but this time he went to the field full of just-ripe cassavas. Silently, he picked enough cassavas for his breakfast, his dinner and for his tea the following day. Pleased with himself, and his arms full of cassavas, Anansi crept back to his hut, where he climbed back into bed and fell fast asleep.

The next day the sun was up again, shining brightly in the sky. This morning the farmer did not need to slip down to the field to gather yams before breakfast as he had brought some with him the night before. Soon he was eating fresh, warm yams, cooked to perfection by his wife. Feeling uneasy, the farmer thought he needed to check his crops, so during breakfast he decided he would go down to his fields, just to ease his mind.

After a short walk down the hill he decided to pick a few of his finest plantains for his meal later that day. He then set about counting his crops and, using pebbles, writing the final counts under the tree. It seemed that he must have counted wrong, so again he counted. He scratched his head. Mmm! Sighing, he realized that when he collected the yams for his tea he had not changed the number. "What an idiot I am," he said to himself, relieved. However, he still felt he should count the cassavas and plantains, just in case.

Soon the cassavas, plantains, and yams were all counted, and then recounted. The farmer checked the number written in pebbles by the large rock on the side of the field. This time he was sure he had counted them correctly, yet the number of cassavas he had was less than the number written with the pebbles. "Who could have done this? What am I to do? I'll go and ask my wife. She's sure to have an idea," said the farmer to himself. So he hurried up to the stream where his wife was washing their clothes. He told her how he had counted the cassavas and placed the number on the ground written in pebbles, so he was sure some had been taken during the night.

"We must catch this thief," she said.

"But how?" asked the farmer. Thinking for a while, the farmer's wife came up with a plan. Soon the farmer was busying himself with his wife's clever plan. He worked all day and by teatime was very tired. After a hearty tea of cassavas, cooked by his wife, he went to bed and slept well.

When the moon had replaced the sun in the sky, Anansi again crept out of bed and down to the farmer's fields. He had done this the night before and the night before that. The first night he had crept down to the field where the yams grew and taken enough for breakfast, dinner and tea. The second night he had taken enough cassavas for breakfast, dinner and tea. Now on the third night he had decided to take a few yams, a few cassavas and a few plantains. Picking a few of only the best yams and placing them under his arm, he then picked a few cassavas. Then Anansi decided he would pick a few of the biggest plantains.

However, to his surprise, there was someone standing at the edge of the field. Wondering who else could be up this time of night, Anansi called out, "Hello there," and waved. The person did not answer. Sighing, Anansi said to himself, "Well, how rude. Perhaps they didn't hear. I'll move closer and try again." Moving closer, Anansi tried again. "Hello," he called. Still the person ignored him. Very annoyed, Anansi decided to go up to the person and tell them just how rude they were.

"Hello there," he said, but the gum doll still made no answer. "Answer me," he said as he nudged the gum doll in the shoulder. The gum doll did not answer and Anansi found his hand was stuck fast. Very annoyed now at the rudeness of this person and that he was stuck, he shouted, "Let me loose or I'll hit you!" The gum doll did not answer, nor did it let him loose. Anansi was now very angry. Looking up into the sky, he began to worry he might be caught as the moon had begun to fall behind the horizon and the sun was beginning to crawl out of bed and into its place in the sky. Anansi dropped the yams and cassavas all around him. "Let me go. Let me go now!" he pleaded. The gum doll still did not answer and still did not let him go. Desperate, Anansi pushed against the gum doll with his foot. "Oh, no!" He was well and truly stuck.

Soon the sun was in the sky and Anansi lowered his head in shame as the farmer came around the corner and found him stuck to the gum doll, for all to see, surrounded by freshly picked yams and cassavas.

What happened next is another story!

• • •

HOW ANANSI GOT TO RIDE TIGER

Anansi was always trying to impress. He was always telling tales of how clever and quick thinking he was, of how he had swum the deepest and widest river, how he had climbed the tallest tree, how he had spun the biggest web, how he could fly like the birds, how he was as strong as the strongest elephant and even how he had ridden Tiger.

One day the chief heard Anansi telling one of his many tales and was amused by the story. He listened intently as Anansi related how he had ridden Tiger. This feat had obviously taken great skill and it also proved just how brave Anansi was, because everyone knew how fierce Tiger was. Having listened to the story, the chief approached Anansi and asked quietly, "Have you really ridden Tiger?"

Anansi puffed out his chest and boasted, "Nana," (because that is what people call their chiefs) "of course, and I am sure I could do it again this afternoon if I wanted to."

However, the chief did not believe Anansi, but was far too nice to say such a thing. So he decided to go and ask Tiger himself, as Tiger was also known for being a truthful creature.

That afternoon the chief went and found Tiger resting in the shade of a tree. As the chief walked up to Tiger, Tiger gave a large yawn, stretched and rose to his feet. "Tiger, I have a question to ask, if I may?" said the chief.

"Nana, of course. You may ask anything," replied Tiger respectfully.

So the chief asked, "Did Anansi really ride you, with a saddle and a bridle?"

Horror-struck at such an idea, Tiger roared, "NO!" Then added, "AND I'll make him take back his words, for they're all lies. I'll bring him to you and you'll hear him apologize to me for such a tale." Turning on his heels, Tiger went to find Anansi.

Now Anansi was not only known for his tales, but also for being a very lazy creature, so Tiger knew exactly where to find him on such a hot day. Soon Tiger found Anansi sitting under a tree by the lake, enjoying the cool breeze as it came in over the water.

"Anansi! Anansi!" shouted Tiger. "You must come with me to see the chief and take back those lies you told this morning."

Anansi looked up meekly. "I'm sorry, Tiger, but I can't come, I'm really ill. That is why I'm resting in the shade of this tree. I can't even walk as I am so weak."

However, Tiger was so angry he would not wait. "You must come with me NOW. I'll not have the chief believe your lies for a moment longer. You must come at once and take back those lies," he roared at Anansi, who still sat in the shade of the tree.

"There is only one way I would be able to see the chief, but you would not hear of it, I am sure," said Anansi, drawing in the sand with his toe.

"Let me decide that," Tiger replied.

"If you take me on your back to the chief, then I'll take back the words. But as I am so weak I would need something to brace my feet against, so I don't fall off," sighed Anansi.

Tiger, blinded by his anger, agreed and after much thought went to borrow a saddle from the farmer and his horse, so Anansi could ride him and take back the lies he had told earlier that very morning.

Tiger returned a little while later, having borrowed a saddle. He found Anansi still in the shade of the tree, but he was now lying on his back looking up through the leaves to the sky beyond. "I'm sorry, Tiger, I'm unable to come with you. I'm feeling even worse and will be unable to ride you to see the chief."

"YOU MUST!" Tiger shouted, because he was sure Anansi was trying to get out of seeing the chief to take back his lies.

"My hands are too weak to hold onto your fur. Without help, I would surely fall off," said Anansi.

Determined he would take Anansi to see the chief so he could take back his lies, Tiger knew exactly what he needed to find.

Tiger soon returned with a bridle he had borrowed from the farmer and his horse. "See, you can ride me now without falling off," said Tiger, showing Anansi the saddle and the bridle. "So come with me NOW to see the chief and take back your lies!" he demanded.

Anansi got to his feet slowly and placed the saddle and bridle on Tiger. Gently, he climbed onto Tiger and was taken to see the chief. As the chief walked out of his hut he was just in time to see Anansi riding Tiger.

• • •

HOW ANANSI TURNED AN EAR OF CORN INTO ONE HUNDRED GOATS

Sometimes when Anansi was bored and had nothing better to do he would dream up ways in which he would be able to prove *just* how clever he really was. Today was just such a day and, as he sat in the shade of the tree by the lake enjoying the cooling breeze, he smiled to himself. He had just come up with a great way to prove how clever he was, so he went to see the chief of the village.

Anansi found the chief sitting in his hut enjoying a meal and talking to his youngest son. "Nana, forgive me, sir, but I was hoping you would be able to give me an ear of corn for my own dinner."

Looking amused, and knowing Anansi would be up to one of his tricks, the chief asked, "And what would I get in return for this ear of corn?"

Appearing to think long and hard, Anansi answered, "Nana, I would repay your kindness and trust by turning this ear of corn into one hundred goats."

Knowing Anansi would never be able to turn an ear of corn into one hundred goats, the chief laughed. Turning to his son, the chief asked, "And what do you think I should do?"

The chief's son thought for a while then replied, "Papa, Anansi is too clever. He would surely not try to fool you." Nodding, the chief turned to Anansi and said, "My son is right: you would not try to fool me, would you, Anansi?"

"Oh, no! You are too kind a chief and too great a man for me to do that!" answered Anansi humbly. So the chief gave Anansi an ear of corn.

Anansi returned home and went to bed early that night so he could put his plan into action the next day.

After a huge breakfast the next morning, Anansi set off with the ear of corn safely packed away in his travel sack. Walking all day, Anansi reached a village just as night began to fall. He went straight to the hut of the chief and knocked loudly.

Now Anansi was good at telling stories and he related a story to the chief, telling him about the ear of corn and how the sky god had given it to him and how he needed somewhere to rest for the night and a place to hide this sacred treasure. The chief was so honored that Anansi should pick his village to stay in that he organized a wonderful banquet in his honor. That night the drummers played, the singers sang and after much food and drink the entire village returned to their huts both happy and very tired.

As the moon rose in the sky and the noises of the night replaced those of the banquet, Anansi crept out of his hut. Under his arm he held the ear of corn tightly and went to the place where the chickens were kept safely each night, throwing the corn into the enclosure. The chickens soon ate the corn and it was gone within minutes. Smiling to himself, Anansi returned to his bed for a good night's sleep.

In the morning Anansi woke up and went to where the corn had been hidden. "Oh, what am I to do?" he shouted as loudly as he could. "Someone has stolen the sacred ear of corn!"

Not believing what he had just heard, the chief ran from his hut. "Surely you are wrong?" he said.

"Look for yourself." Anansi pointed at the hiding place. "You saw me place the ear of corn there and now it is gone!" The chief could see Anansi was right, the corn had gone. Scared the sky god would bring misfortune to his village, the chief gave Anansi a bushel of corn to replace the ear that had been stolen in the night. Anansi thanked the chief and told him the sky god would also be grateful for his generosity, then left on his journey.

Now a bushel of corn is very heavy and Anansi was not used to hard work, so he carried it for as long as he could, which was not for very long. Soon he needed a rest and sat by the roadside so he could watch the world go by. A man carrying a chicken walked past on his way to market. Anansi called the man over and they were soon swapping. Anansi gave the man his bushel of corn and Anansi received the chicken in return. Luckily for Anansi, a chicken is far lighter to carry than a bushel of corn so he set off on his way again.

Anansi walked all day and by nightfall reached the next

village. He went straight to the hut of the chief and knocked loudly. Now, as we know, Anansi was good at telling stories and he related his story well. He told the chief about the chicken he was carrying, how the sky god had given it to him and how he needed a place to rest for the night. The chief was so honored that Anansi should pick his village to stay, that in his honor he put on a wonderful banquet. Well into the night the food was eaten, songs were sung and the drums were played. When the villagers, the chief and Anansi had eaten all the food, sung all the songs and danced until they could dance no more they all returned to their huts both happy and very tired.

As the moon rose in the sky and the noises of the night replaced those of the banquet, Anansi crept out of the hut he had been given to stay in. He killed the chicken and covered the ground outside the chief's hut with feathers and blood. Smiling to himself, Anansi returned to his bed for a good night's sleep.

In the morning Anansi awoke and went to the place where the chicken had been hidden. "What am I to do?" he shouted. "Someone has stolen the sacred chicken!"

The chief ran from his hut. "Surely you are wrong?" he said.

"Look for yourself." Anansi pointed at the hiding place. "You saw me tether the chicken here and now it is gone!" The chief could see Anansi was right: the chicken had gone. Then Anansi pointed at the chief's hut in disbelief. There on the ground around the hut was blood and feathers. Knowing he had not killed the chicken, but also knowing that it looked as if he had, the chief was worried the sky god would send misfortune to his village. So he gave Anansi ten of his best sheep as compensation. Anansi thanked the chief and left on his journey.

Now herding sheep is very tiring if, like Anansi, you are not used to work, so after a short while Anansi stopped by the roadside. As he watched the world go by he noticed a man struggling to put the body of a dead man onto the back of his cart. Always being a nosy creature, Anansi went to ask him what he was doing. The man explained that this was a stranger who had died the night before and he was taking him to church so he could be blessed. Anansi praised him for being such a kind soul, then added he knew the man and that he was a friend from a distant village. Asking if he could buy his cart for ten sheep, Anansi told him he could then take his friend's body home. The man was more than willing to sell his cart for ten good sheep and Anansi soon found himself on the road again.

Anansi travelled all day and by nightfall reached a new village. He went straight to the hut of the chief and knocked loudly. Now Anansi, being good at telling stories, related a story to the chief, telling him how the man sleeping in the back of the cart was the son of a great and good sky god and how they both needed a place to rest for the night. The chief was so honored that Anansi should pick his village to stay in that he laid on a wonderful banquet. The drums were brought out and the drummers played, the singers sang and a special show was put on where fire was eaten and acrobats performed great feats of daring. That night the entire village returned to their huts both happy and very tired.

In the morning Anansi awoke and ran from his hut to the chief's. "I am unable to wake the sky god's son, please help me!" he cried. The villagers, after much discussion, decided to sing and play music as loudly as they could. So they played all the tunes they knew and sang all the songs they knew as loudly as they could. Yet they were unable to wake the man. Desperate, they pounded on his chest to wake him. Anansi then pulled everyone back. "Oh, no, you have killed him! What am I to do?"

The terrified villagers asked what could they do to show the sky god just how sorry they were. Thinking hard and long, Anansi said, "One hundred goats is what is needed!"

• • •

HOW ANANSI WON THE
STORIES OF THE SKY GOD

Anansi sat under a tree and sighed slowly; he was so bored. He had nothing to do, nothing to occupy his mind. He folded his arms and wished he could have one of the stories owned by the sky god, Nyamse.

You see at this time Nyamse the Sky God kept all the stories hidden away from view and never let anyone tell them, read them or even see them. So there were no books, no films, no television, no songs and no dreams. Because, however you look at it, these are all stories and all the stories were hidden away.

As he lay there Anansi wondered how it would feel to own the stories himself. He grinned. Oh, how jealous everyone would be if he owned the stories of the sky god. How he could boast and how he would enjoy telling everyone all the stories he owned and of course the story of how he got them in the first place. It was then Anansi decided to see if the sky god would sell them to him and what price he would ask. So Anansi packed himself some food and set off to the home of the sky god, Nyamse.

Travelling for days, he finally came to the place where

the sky god lived and asked Nyamse what he would take as payment for his stories. Considering long and hard, Nyamse replied, "The price to be paid will be great. Many have tried to buy my stories, but no one has yet met my price. All I ask in return for my stories is the hornets, a python, one of the fairies and a leopard. If you can bring these to me I'll give you all the stories told so far and all the stories yet to be told."

"I'll get them, get them all!" promised Anansi.

Returning home, Anansi found his wife in the kitchen washing and preparing food, which she was then storing in a selection of her finest pots. He told his wife, Aso, what the sky god had said. "But how on earth can I get what he asks for?" Scratching his chin, he added, "And how on earth can I catch the hornets? Everyone knows how bad-tempered they are. If I try to trick them, well, I hate to imagine what they would do." Thinking for a while as she brushed away the embers from the fire, Anansi's wife told him what to do.

"You are clever. I'll follow your plan."

So Anansi took a gourd and filled it with water. Next he went to the place where the hornets were. Sprinkling himself with water, he cried, "Oh, it's raining! Where can I shelter?" He knew how much the hornets hated the rain. Looking around, he saw a banana tree and took a large leaf from it so he could shelter under it. Again he sprinkled himself with water. Seeing the hornets, he went over to them. "Can't you see it's raining? Why do you think I'm hiding under this leaf?" he asked them. "If you want shelter you can hide from the rain in this gourd if you want." Thanking him, the hornets flew into the hollow gourd. Quickly he covered the hole. "There, I have you! Now I can give you to the sky god as some of the payment for his stories," said Anansi happily.

After Anansi had taken the hornets to the sky god, and promised he would get him Python, returning home he found his wife, Aso, making pots from the clay she had dug out of the earth a few days earlier. You see, making clay pots requires soft delicate hands, with a gentle touch, and Aso was a fine pot maker. Anansi told his wife what the sky god had said. "But how on earth can I get what he asks for?" Anansi asked her.

As she made her pot Aso thought hard, then came up with a clever plan to trick Onini the Python. Anansi knew how vain Onini was, so was sure his wife's plan would work. Picking up his hatchet, he walked into the forest and, seeking the longest, straightest branch he could find, he chopped it down.

Muttering loudly to himself, making sure everyone in the forest could hear what he was saying, Anansi said, "Wife, you are so wrong, and I'll prove it!" Then Anansi went to find the python as he lazed on a nearby rock, warming himself under the hot sun.

"Aso, this branch is definitely longer than the python. I can't believe you think it is shorter. Anyone can see just how wrong you are, and I'm going to prove it," said Anansi to himself, just loud enough to make sure the snake could hear. "How can you say this branch is shorter? It makes no sense."

The python, being a vain creature, overheard Anansi muttering to himself and slid over to him. "What's that you say, Anansi? Is it true your wife thinks that the branch you are carrying is shorter than me? Is she a fool?"

"She asked me to go into the forest and cut a branch for her which is longer than you. This is the branch I cut," explained Anansi, holding out the branch for Onini to see. "I told her this was definitely longer than you, but she said I was wrong and that it is shorter."

"She is wrong!" replied Onini, firmly nodding his head as he spoke.

"Python," Anansi said, "my wife, Aso, has really wound me up. Will you help prove her wrong?"

Agreeing to help, the python watched as Anansi laid the branch on the ground. Onini then lay on the ground next to the branch, but to his horror found he was slightly shorter.

"We must prove she is wrong or I'll never live it down," said Anansi. "I'll tie your tail to the end of the branch so you can stretch out further and become longer than it is."

Now, being a very vain creature and not wanting Anansi's wife to be right, Onini agreed to let Anansi tie his tail to the branch. Stretching out as far as he could, the python found he was still shorter than the branch.

"I have an idea," said Anansi. "Let me tie your middle too so you can stretch even further." Well, being a very vain creature and not wanting Anansi's wife to be right, the python let Anansi tie his middle. Again he stretched just that little bit more, pulling against the ropes that bound him to the branch. Finally, he was as long as the branch, but, before he could ask Anansi to let him go, Anansi had tied his neck to the branch.

"There, I have you! Now I can give you to the sky god as some of the payment for his stories," said Anansi with a smile.

After Anansi had taken the python to the sky god and promised he would get him one of the fairies, Anansi sat eating a bowl of yams. Scratching his head, he asked his wife, "How on earth will I catch one of the fairies? They are all so quick, flitting here and there, one of them will never stay still long enough for me to catch her." Thinking for a while as she washed the dishes, Anansi's wife told him what to do.

"You're clever. I'll follow your plan," said Anansi approvingly.

That morning Anansi busied himself tapping the gum tree for some sticky gum. He made himself a doll, which he covered with the gum. Tying a string around her waist, he then put her beneath the odum tree (which was where the fairies played) with a bowl of mashed yams, which was not only his favorite food but also the favorite of the fairies. Hiding in the bush, Anansi waited for a fairy to come out and play. He waited so long that he fell asleep. Just as the sun went down he was awoken by a sweet voice asking, "Is that mashed yams in your bowl? That is my favorite. Can I have a little?"

Realizing it was a fairy talking to his gum doll, Anansi

pulled on the string. The gum doll nodded her head and the fairy took the bowl and ate her fill of mashed yams. The fairy being polite, if not a little greedy, thanked the doll. This time Anansi didn't pull on the thread. The doll ignored the fairy. "Well, how rude," said the fairy and repeated herself. Again the doll did not answer. Thinking the doll must have fallen asleep, the fairy prodded her in the shoulder. Her hand stuck fast. "Let me go, let me go!" cried the fairy as she tried with the other hand to get herself unstuck.

Quickly, Anansi jumped out of the bush. "Great, I have you! Now I can give you to the sky god as payment for his stories," he said joyfully.

Soon after Anansi had taken the fairy to the sky god and promised he would get him a leopard, Anansi sat under the shade of a tree fanning himself with a leaf. "Wife, how will I ever catch the leopard? They are so fast I'll never be able to chase one and catch it." Thinking for a while, Anansi's wife told him what to do.

"You're clever. I'll follow your plan."

All that day in the forest Anansi busied himself with his wife's plan and that night he slept well. In the morning he did not even wait for his breakfast, but ran out into the forest to see if his trap had worked. Sure enough, deep in the pit Anansi had dug the day before, sulked Osebo the Leopard. Hiding his happiness, Anansi looked over the edge of the pit. "Oh, Osebo, I'm so sorry. It wasn't you I wanted to catch. I'll help you out. Just give me a moment to get some branches for you to climb up." Osebo was so angry he didn't answer Anansi, but simply growled his displeasure.

Anansi pulled out two long straight branches he had cut the day before. Now these were no ordinary branches as they were covered with gum from the gum tree. Careful to touch only the ends of the branches, as they did not have gum on them, Anansi lowered them into the pit. The leopard was so eager to get out of the pit that he didn't check the branches and quickly jumped onto them. To his dismay, all four paws were stuck fast.

"There, I have you. Now I can give you to the sky god as part payment for his stories," Anansi almost sang.

When Anansi took the leopard to the sky god, the god was amazed Anansi had managed to get all he had asked for. All the great kings and chiefs had failed to get the hornets, a python, one of the fairies and a leopard, but Anansi had managed it. As he gave the stories over he told Anansi that from that day onwards all stories would be called Anansesem, spider stories in honor of Anansi and his great deeds.

Very, very happy, Anansi returned home. However, in his haste to return home and because he was not looking where he was going, Anansi tripped and fell. Now, as he was coming home from the place where the sky god lived Anansi fell from a very great height and as he fell, so did the pot containing all the stories he had just won. As the pot fell to earth the lid came off and all the stories fell out. The wind caught them and scattered them to the four corners of the world.

So luckily we can now go to the pictures or sit in front of the television watching our favorite program. If Anansi had not taken a tumble and all the stories had not fallen out of the pot and the wind had not caught them, then we would have to ask him! Could you think of anything worse?

• • •

WHY SPIDERS STAY ON THE CEILING

As per usual, Anansi was boasting about all the great things he had done and just how clever he was. He boasted how he could make a web to catch his dinner, a thing nobody else could do; everyone else had to catch their dinner by chasing it or finding it. He was so clever his meals came to him. He boasted how he had won the stories of the sky god, Nyamse, and how he had then been so generous by giving them to the world (although we know different, don't we?). How he had the ability to turn a simple ear of corn into one hundred goats. Yes, one hundred goats! Who would have believed it?

As Anansi boasted on and on, the king of all the beasts, Lion, sighed a great sigh and shook his head slowly. Lion was SO fed up with Anansi and all of his boasting that he went to Eagle and asked, "How can we teach Anansi the spider a lesson? He's always on about how clever he is. He can't be that clever. He is driving me up the wall. We really need to teach him a lesson, before he drives me completely mad!"

Thinking for a while, Eagle said, "I'll ask Anansi a simple question and, being so boastful, he's sure to want to prove himself." So Eagle and Lion went to the tree where Anansi had made his web and Eagle asked, "Anansi, if you're so clever why can't you fly like the birds?"

Puffing out his chest, Anansi replied, "Of course I can fly. What a silly question."

"I would love to see you fly, Anansi," Lion butted in. "Perhaps in a week you'll be able to show me how well you can."

Not wanting to look a fool in front of the king of beasts, Anansi agreed to the challenge set by Eagle and the king himself. He sat and thought for a very long time, wondering how he would prove just how well he could fly. When he came up with a plan, Anansi set about collecting feathers from all the birds. He asked if he could have a few feathers from Vulture and a few more from Hornbill and a few more yet from the ox-peckers, both the yellow-billed and the red-billed. He even had the cheek to ask Eagle, who gave him a couple of his finest and longest flight feathers. Anansi then went to the gum tree and cut into its bark. The gum oozed from the tree and Anansi collected it in a bowl. Soon he was ready to show just how good a flyer he really was.

The day came for Anansi to meet the challenge set by Eagle and Lion. All the other animals had heard about it so came to watch as Anansi stuck the feathers onto his body with the gum. Soon he was ready and he climbed to the top of the tallest tree. He jumped into the air and surprised even himself when he found he was actually flying. Eagle flew beside him, egging him on and on. The air ruffled

Eagle's feathers as he flew. "Anansi, you can actually fly, and quite well at that. But can you keep up with me?"

Full of confidence, Anansi shouted over the noise of the wind, "I can fly wherever you can, Eagle. Take me wherever you dare."

Circling to catch the currents of warm air as they rose from the land far below, Eagle was transported higher and higher into the sky. Anansi, determined to follow Eagle, rode the air too and soon the animals below grew smaller and smaller, becoming little dots below them. As they rose into the sky Anansi was so pleased with himself he didn't notice how close the sun was and how hot it had become. Soon the land below them was just a mosaic of color. It was then Anansi saw how the gum was melting and how the feathers were coming away, one by one, gently fluttering back down to earth. Before Anansi had time to react almost all the feathers were gone.

Anansi found himself falling to earth. "Oh, noooooo!" he shouted as he saw the ground coming towards him faster and faster, much faster than he had left it. The clouds rushed past him as the last feather fell from his body. As he looked down he saw he was about to land on the roof of the farmer's house. The animals had seen what had happened and how Eagle had tricked Anansi. They rushed to the house and reached it just as Anansi hit the roof with a loud thump. Anansi lay there for a minute, pleased to find nothing was harmed, except for his pride. He was so embarrassed that he had been tricked by Eagle that he refused to leave the roof he had just landed on and said he would stay on the ceiling forever!

• • •

ANANSI AND THE WITCH NAMED 'FIVE'

In a village near to where Anansi lived, there lived a witch. She was a very old, grumpy witch who had many great powers and who didn't like people very much, so nobody annoyed her, just in case! This witch was called (shhh, now whisper this name, just in case!) Five. The grumpy old witch hated her name and Anansi had overheard her saying, "If anyone dare say my name, I'll make them disappear in a puff of smoke. Where they go, no one will ever know. But they will be gone, and gone forever!"

Now it was known by all that Anansi was a lazy creature and would not go hunting for food if he could possibly avoid it, preferring that it either came to him or to take it from others. He would often try to come up with clever ways to feed himself and his family with as little effort as possible on his part. So when he heard the witch saying she would make anyone who said her name disappear, he thought of a very clever plan.

Anansi busied himself by collecting five pieces of corn, which did not take him very long at all. Wrapping the corn in a piece of cloth, he walked to the main road, which led to the market. Today was market day, which meant the road was very busy. So Anansi sat himself down under the shade of a tree and opened the cloth and placed the corn pieces in a row. One, two, three, four, (shhh), *five!*

He watched as the world passed him by, looking forward to the food he would soon earn himself. After an hour or so of sitting there his friend Rabbit stopped to talk to Anansi. Now Rabbit was carrying a large sack of fresh, ripe yams, cassavas, and plantains. They were all ready for sale at the market. "What have you there, Anansi?" asked Rabbit.

"Oh, just some corn. Would you like some?" replied Anansi.

"I only have this to sell. I don't have any money," said Rabbit, holding up his large sack.

Making it look like he was thinking hard, Anansi said, "Well, if you tell me how many pieces of corn I have, I'll give you one."

"You're trying to trick me!"

"No, no! Just count how many pieces of corn I have and I promise to give you the last one you count."

Wondering what Anansi was up to, Rabbit counted out the number of pieces of corn. He was sure simply counting pieces of corn could do no harm, and after all, Anansi had just promised. "One, two, three, four, five."

Puff!

In a large ball of smoke Rabbit disappeared and the food he had been carrying in the sack had fallen out and now lay on the ground scattered around Anansi's feet. Rubbing his hands together with glee, Anansi picked up the food and put it on the cloth with the corn. Wrapping all the food up, Anansi returned home and his wife was soon busy in the kitchen cooking.

Within a few days the food was all eaten and Aso, Anansi's wife, was soon complaining there was nothing for her to cook. "Don't worry, I'll go and earn myself some food so you can cook me a wonderful meal," he said.

Anansi collected his five pieces of corn wrapped in the cloth and walked to the main road, which led to the market. The day being market day meant the road was very busy. So Anansi sat himself down under the shade of a tree, opened the cloth and placed the corn in a row. One, two, three, four, (*shhh*), five. Anansi watched as the world passed him by and within a few minutes Rhino appeared, carrying food in a large sack, which he was going to sell at the market. "Hi, Anansi, what do you have there?" he asked.

"Oh, just some corn. Would you like some?" replied Anansi.

"I don't have any money. I'm going to the market to sell, not buy," said Rhino.

"Well, if you tell me how many pieces of corn I have, I'll give you a piece," replied Anansi.

"You're trying to trick me!"

"No, no! Just count how many pieces of corn I have and I promise to give you the last one you count."

So Rhino counted out the number of pieces of corn lying on the cloth. "One, two, three, four, five."

Woof!

Rhino disappeared in a large ball of smoke and the food

he had been carrying now lay on the ground scattered all around. Anansi picked it up and put it on the cloth with the corn. Wrapping all the food up, Anansi returned home and his wife was soon busy in the kitchen cooking.

Again, within a few days all the food was gone and Aso was soon complaining there was nothing for her to cook. "I'll go and earn myself some food for you to cook. Don't worry," Anansi told her. Anansi then collected his five pieces of corn wrapped in the cloth and walked to the main road, which led to the market.

The day was market day and that meant the road was very busy. Anansi sat himself down under the shade of a tree and opened the cloth and placed the corn in a row next to him. One, two, three, four (*shhh*), *five*. Anansi wondered who he would be able to trick today. After ten minutes or so Goat passed by and stopped to talk to Anansi. She was carrying with her a sack full of food. "Hello, Anansi, what have you there?" she asked.

"Just some corn I can't be bothered to carry to market," he replied. "Would you like to buy some?"

"Oh, I'm not buying today, Anansi. I'm going to market to sell."

"Oh, well if you can count my corn, I'll give you the last piece you count," Anansi told her.

Knowing Anansi was not only lazy but also liked to play tricks on people, Goat guessed he was up to something. "Well, let me see," she said. "You have one piece, two pieces, three, four and that piece right next to you." She pointed.

"No, no. You have to count them all, one at a time."

Goat smiled. "Well, let me try again. You have one, two, three, four and the piece of corn by your foot."

"No, no. Did you not hear me just count them all, one at a time?"

Goat smiled an even bigger smile. "Let me try once more then. One, two, three, four and the piece of corn by your foot."

Anansi was now very annoyed that Goat could not count. "No! Don't you see, there are one, two three, four, FIVE ..."

Whoops!!!!

. . .

ANANSI AND THE POT OF WISDOM

A long, long time ago when the earth was young and so were all the other creatures, wisdom was kept in a large clay pot, which had three little feet and a very tight-fitting lid. Anansi looked after this pot and when any of the others animals in the jungle needed help with making a decision or solving a problem, they would visit Anansi. They would turn up at any time during the day and sometimes during the night as well. They would ask him to look in the pot and see if the pot of wisdom was able to help them solve their problem.

Well, in the beginning Anansi would puff out his chest and make a big fuss that it was *he* who was in charge of looking after the pot of wisdom. It was *he* who looked in the pot to get the answers the other animals wanted. But as time went on Anansi got fed up with all the animals visiting; he enjoyed lazing around in the shadow of a tree far more than helping the other animals.

Take one day last week, for example: the sun had just climbed into the sky and one of Rabbit's children hopped up to see Anansi. "Anansi, please look in the pot for me. My brothers and sisters tease me because I'm scared of the night."

Anansi took the pot with three little legs and a tight-fitting lid down from the shelf and opened it. Now when the pot answered it would not give a simple answer like, "Oh, don't be silly, there is nothing that can harm you." It would answer by using either a riddle or an old African proverb. As always the pot gave its answer: "no matter how long the night, the day is sure to come." Thinking for a while, Rabbit's child thanked Anansi for looking in the pot and returned to his burrow no longer scared of the night.

Anansi then began to cook his breakfast when he heard a buzzing outside his door. Tutting, because he was getting hungry, he went over to the door and opened it. One of the worker bees from the nearby beehive hovered in front of him. "Ananzzi, pleazz look in the pot of wizzdom for me. My sisters and I have heard of a tree far away that izz in full bloom and will be full of nectar. But we are scared our little wingzz will not carry uzz that far."

Sighing loudly, Anansi walked over to the shelf where the little pot of wisdom with three little legs and a tight-fitting lid lived and opened it. As always the pot came up with an answer: "if an opportunity is not taken, it passes away." "Thank you," buzzed the little worker bee and returned to her hive to tell her sisters the answer the pot had given.

Now Anansi was just about to sit down and eat his breakfast under the shade of a tree when Leopard Cub bounced into view. "Anansi, look in the pot of wisdom for me. My mum says I must join in the hunt. But I'm scared I won't be strong enough and fast enough for the chase."

Huffing, Anansi put his breakfast down and went into the house to get the little pot with the three small legs and the tight-fitting lid. Bringing it out into the warm sun, Anansi opened the pot and out came the wisdom: "the harder the chase, the better the catch." Thinking about this answer for a while, the leopard cub thanked Anansi for looking in it and returned to his mother now ready and eager to join in the hunt.

And so the day went on. At lunchtime Tiger came along, just before his afternoon nap, and asked for the wisdom pot to be consulted. In the afternoon Turtle came to seek the advice of the pot (even though he had started out in the morning, it had taken Turtle all this time to get to Anansi's home). At teatime Hippo came to seek the help of the pot of wisdom. When the sun went down Bat climbed out of his bed, flew to Anansi's house and asked Anansi to open the lid of the pot and seek the wisdom that was hidden inside.

So, you see, day or night the creatures of the jungle would need the wisdom held within the pot Anansi looked after. Anansi felt like he spent his entire life taking the little pot with three small legs and a tight-fitting lid down from the shelf and consulting it.

Then one morning, after Anansi had spent hours looking in the pot for Elephant, Lion, Snake, Zebra, the hornets, Antelope, Turtle for a second time (because by the time he got home he had forgotten the answer and had to come back and ask the question again) and even his wife, Aso, Anansi decided he would hide the pot in the tallest tree and tell everyone that the pot had been stolen. At least that way he would get some rest.

So Anansi spun a silken thread around the pot so the lid would not come off, then tied the thread around his neck. As he walked to the base of the tallest tree the pot kept bouncing on Anansi's stomach. He stood at the bottom of the tree and slowly began to climb. With every step he took the pot bounced against his stomach and the trunk of the tree. Muttering some very naughty words, Anansi clumsily slid back down the tree. Just then Anansi's oldest son, Etikelenkele, (which means big-headed) walked past. "Papa, what are you doing?" he asked.

"Never you mind!" Anansi snapped back at Etikelenkele, angry that he had not managed to hide the pot of wisdom. "Leave your poor ol' papa alone."

So Etikelenkele left his papa sitting beneath the cooling branches of the tree. After a while Anansi took the pot off and shortened the thread that was around his neck. "That should do it!" he told himself and once again began to climb the tree. Again the pot bounced between the trunk of the tree and Anansi's stomach. Again Anansi muttered some bad words and scolded himself for not being able to get the pot up the tree. He slid back down to the base of the tree and sat beneath its cooling cover. Just then Anansi's second son, Nankonwhia, (which means thin-legged) wandered past.

"Papa, what are you doing?" he asked.

"Never you mind!" Anansi snapped back at Nankonwhia, angry that he had not managed to hide the pot of wisdom. "Leave your poor ol' papa alone." So Nankonwhia left his papa sitting in the shade of the tree.

Thinking for a little while longer, Anansi decided to untie the pot and hold it under his many arms. But as he tried to climb the tree he found he needed all his arms and legs to hold onto the trunk. Sliding down the tree trunk again and muttering some really naughty words this time, he sat down and sighed. Anansi was sure he would never be able to hide the pot of wisdom. As Anansi was sitting beneath the branches of the tallest tree his third son, Ntikuma, (which means small-headed) came by. "Papa, what are you doing?" he asked.

"Never you mind!" Anansi snapped back at Ntikuma, angry that he had not managed to hide the pot of wisdom. "Leave your poor ol' papa alone." So Ntikuma left his papa to sit in the shade of the tree.

Anansi decided to give it one last go. So he tied the pot around his waist in front of him, securely fastening the silken thread. As he wobbled towards the tree, he heard laughter behind him. Spinning around, Anansi saw his fourth son, Afudutwedotwe, (which means big stomach) laughing at his papa. "And I thought it was my name which meant big stomach, not yours!"

Anansi was not amused that his son was laughing at him and growled, "Don't laugh at me!"

Hiding a large grin behind his hand, Afudutwedotwe asked, "But Papa, what are you doing?"

"I'm trying to take the pot of wisdom to the top of this tree," he said, pointing up through the branches, then added, "Because I'm fed up with answering everyone's silly questions and just want to have a little rest"

"Then why don't you tie it to your back?" asked Anansi's youngest son.

Anansi was so angry with himself for not thinking of this that he took the pot and threw it to the ground. As the little clay pot with three small legs and a tight-fitting lid hit the ground it smashed into a thousand pieces. Then just as luck would have it, a large gust of wind caught the wisdom and carried it to the four corners of the world.

So now wisdom is shared by all and luckily we don't have to go and ask Anansi to open up the pot and take a little look inside. Phew!

• • •

ANANSI AND THE TOMMY
(THOMPSON GAZELLE)

One bright sunny morning Anansi awoke from his slumber to find the tree he had made his web in gently swaying back and forth. Now we all know just how clever Anansi is, so it is not surprising he knew this was not caused by the wind, and he knew it was not caused by rain. You may be wondering how he knew this. It was because the whole tree was moving, not just the leaves. So he carefully parted the leaves to see what was causing his tree to move.

To his horror he could see flames in the distance, looking like they were right at the edge of the world. But they were travelling fast and sending up great flashes of yellow, orange and red, filling the sky with their color. As the trees and bushes burnt, a huge cloud of smoke drifted up into the cloudless sky. However, Anansi knew it was not the bush fire that was making his tree gently sway. It was the many animals rushing below his tree to get away from the spreading flames that were making his tree move.

Anansi sat in his tree, safe from harm, watching the animals as they ran beneath, running for their lives as the flames ate the savannah and crept closer and closer. The family of elephants thundered past, calling to one another with loud blasts from their trunks to make sure the little ones were not left behind. Zebras streaked past, their stripes becoming a blur in the dust cloud created by the many running feet and hooves. The giraffe family galloped past on their long legs, dodging around the small trees and under the tall ones, bending their long necks down so they did not get their heads tangled in the leaves and branches. Even Leopard ran from the flames, making great leaps and bounds with his powerful legs as he tried not to trip over the other animals and the twisted roots of trees and rocks peeking up from the ground. All the animals were heading towards the safety of the river, away from the flames, which consumed everything in their path.

As Anansi watched the rumpus below he became aware that the air was becoming warm and smelt of burnt leaves, flowers and bark. "I must get away before the flames take me too." However he knew his small, very hairy legs would never be able to carry him fast enough to avoid the flames as they marched across the land. So he called out, "Who will carry me away from the flames?" But no one heard him over the noise of the running feet and hooves. "Please, will someone carry me away to the safety of the river?" Anansi called out again.

As luck would have it (and Anansi always seems to have luck on his side, when he really needs it!) a herd of Thompson Gazelles, known by all as Tommys, had just reached the shade of Anansi's tree. By chance one of the females heard him above her head and shouted up,

"Anansi, Spider man, if you are quick and jump onto my head I will carry you."

In a flash Anansi jumped from his spot in the tree and tied himself securely around the tip of one of the Tommy's small horns. As the Tommy ran Anansi was able to see any obstacles which were in her way, because, you see, he was higher than her eyes and could see further. He shouted in her ear, "Tommy, run to the left, otherwise a fallen branch will trip you up." The Tommy veered to the left and dodged the fallen branch just in time.

"Tommy, behind the tree stump which is coming up is a small rock. Leap as high and as far as you can," shouted Anansi over the din of the other animals running. So Tommy mustered up all her energy and jumped as high and as far as she could. As her four feet touched the ground they just missed the rock.

Again from his vantage point on her horn, Anansi shouted as loudly as he could, "Tommy, don't try to cross the river here. I can see Hippo guarding his stretch of river and he's not happy, as many have already crossed here. Try further down." So the Tommy followed the riverbank for a short while and crossed where the bank on the other side was easy to climb. When they reached the other side, the Tommy was exhausted and fell to the ground, gasping for breath, her chest heaving in and out with each huge gasp. Anansi untied himself from her horn and sat beside her. They watched the flames reach the bank and slowly die as they had nowhere else to go and nothing else to feed on.

One year later, the rains had washed away the embers of

the great fire and the savannah was now covered with a hundred different greens. Light greens, dark greens, even greens with a hint of yellow. The grass had begun to grow back and the trees were covered in fresh, sweet leaves. Most of the animals had returned to their homes and had forgotten the great fire which had forced them from their homes the year before. New life was everywhere; even the Tommy had given birth to a new fawn.

The Tommy cared for her new baby, as any good mother would. However, on this day she sniffed the air and gasped: she could smell man. Carefully creeping from her hiding place beneath a bush, she watched in horror as she realized the men were hunters! She needed to run away, but her fawn was not strong enough to outrun them. What was she to do?

Anansi had also seen the hunters from the branches of his tree. He had not forgotten the great fire and how the Tommy had helped him to escape the burning yellow, orange and red flames. Dropping from his web high in his tree, Anansi scampered over to the Tommy on his eight very hairy legs. "Run, run for your life and I will protect your baby."

"How can you protect my baby from the hunters?" she asked, then added, "You're just a spider."

"Trust me. If you hadn't helped me when the flames took our homes I would not be able to repay you today," answered Anansi.

Knowing she had no choice, the Tommy ran, ran as fast as she could, dodging the twisted roots of the trees and the rocks that littered the ground. The hunters saw her running away and knew they would not be able to catch her. But they also knew that this was the time of year for babies and that the Tommy must have left her fawn hidden in the bushes. All they had to do was find it and they would be sure of a feast tonight. They looked under many bushes and were soon very close to where the fawn lay hidden. "Stay still, my little one," Anansi told the fawn. "They'll not find you."

Anansi busied himself making the biggest web he had ever made in his life. He spun like he had never spun before. He jumped from branch to branch, covering the bush with his silken thread, which glistened in the rays of the sun. As the hunters neared the bush, they noticed Anansi working away. They laughed at the web he was making. One of the hunters laughed and pointed. "Boy, he must be hungry. Look at that large web he's making. He must want to catch a Tommy for himself."

After searching beneath all the bushes except the one Anansi had spun his web around, as they didn't want to become ensnared in its sticky threads, the hunters decided they would have to look somewhere else. Anansi climbed back into his tree and watched the hunters as they disappeared into the haze of the day. That night the Tommy cautiously returned to the bush where she had left her baby hidden. To her surprise it was covered with the biggest web she had ever seen. It was so thick and so big that she could not see her baby. "Anansi! Anansi!" she cried.

Dropping from the tree, Anansi sat grinning at her as he sat on top of the biggest web he had ever spun.

"Where is my baby?" the Tommy asked Anansi, on the verge of tears.

"Don't worry, Tommy, I hid your baby from the hunters as I promised."

"But where?" The Tommy looked around, confused.

Slowly, Anansi began to unravel the web he had spun around the bush. As he did the Tommy carefully watched. She did not believe Anansi could have hidden her baby so well. As the last strand was removed from the branches of the bush, the baby Tommy trotted out of his protective cover and began to suckle on his mother's milk.

As the mother fed her baby Anansi slipped back up into his web, happy he had repaid his debt.

• • •

HOW ANANSI MISSED FOUR
PARTIES ON ONE NIGHT

Anansi loves to go to parties. The problem is, he doesn't get invited to many. The animals are so used to his tricks that they tend to forget to invite him. But this doesn't stop Anansi inviting himself and going anyway.

Now one day as Anansi sat in his web enjoying the warmth of the sun, he noticed some of the animals chatting under the great meeting tree. Anansi was sure they were planning something fun. So he crept down from his web and hid behind a nearby bush so he could listen. Unfortunately, the bush wasn't near enough and the only thing Anansi managed to overhear was the word 'party'.

"A party," said Anansi. "How am I going to find out who is holding it and when? I'll have to sit here and listen all day."

So Anansi sat hidden behind the bush. But when Rabbit and Turtle were talking the wind whisked their voices away and Anansi missed everything they said. When Hippo and Hyena were talking Goat was noisily munching on the bush's sweet leaves. When Lion and Eagle were talking Frog started to croak and her huge croak drowned out

Lion's and Eagle's voices.

Anansi sighed. "At this rate I'll never find out who's having a party. I may as well go back to my web."

Creeping back to his web, Anansi thought about how he could find out when the next party was happening. Finally, he smiled and called some of his children.

Now," he told them, "the other animals are planning a party and I don't want to miss it. I want you to find out who is going to have a party and when."

"Yes, Papa," replied Anansi's children.

Anansi waited and waited, but his children didn't come back. Just as the sun was setting Anansi was about to give up when his eldest son returned.

"Papa, I overheard Rabbit planning a party, but he can't decide when to have it," he said.

"You're a good son," said Anansi. "Come and find me tomorrow. I have a small task for you."

Just as his eldest son was leaving his youngest son returned.

"Papa, I overheard Eagle planning a party, but he's not decided when it will be."

"You're a good son," said Anansi. "Come and find me tomorrow. I have a small task for you."

As his youngest son was leaving his eldest daughter returned.

"Papa, I overheard Hippo planning a party, but I didn't find out when."

"You're a good daughter," said Anansi. "Find me tomorrow. I have a small task for you."

As the moon was taking its place in the sky Anansi's middle son returned. "Papa, I overheard Lion planning a party, but I didn't find out when."

"You're a good son," said Anansi. "Find me tomorrow. I have a task for you."

The next day, as the sun was peeking over the horizon, Anansi called his children to him.

"I can't miss going to a party," he told them. "So each of you take one of these silken threads. I'll tie them around my middle. When you discover when a party is about to start, pull on the thread and I'll follow it."

Anansi's children each took hold of a silken thread and floated off on the warm morning breeze. Anansi's eldest son went to find out when Rabbit was having his party. Anansi's middle son went to discover when Lion was going to have his party. Anansi's daughter went to find out when Hippo was going to have her party and his youngest son went to find out when Eagle was going to have his.

Anansi crept into the middle of his web and smiled. "Now there's no way I'll miss a party."

As Anansi slept the day away he dreamt of all the parties he was going to attend. He dreamt about Rabbit's party, about Eagle's party, about Lion's party and about Hippo's party. He dreamt about all the lovely food there would be to eat and the wonderful music he would listen to.

The day slowly passed as Anansi slept. The sun began to sink below the horizon and the moon and stars began to fill the sky. Anansi woke from his slumber, stretched and yawned.

"I wonder when the parties will be?" Anansi asked himself.

Suddenly one of the silken threads jerked.

"Ouch!" said Anansi, grabbing the thread. "I can't breathe, but if I cut it I'll not know where the party will be."

The thread jerked again, becoming tighter.

"Oh my," said Anansi. "I can't breathe. I'll have to cut the thread. At least I'll still have three threads left. I'll go to one of those parties instead."

Anansi cut the thread and as he did he breathed a sigh of relief. "That's better," he said, with a smile.

As he settled back down a second thread was pulled.

"A party is about to start," said Anansi happily. "I wonder whose it is?"

The second thread was pulled again, "Ouch," said Anansi, "that hurts!" Suddenly the third thread was pulled. "Oh my," wheezed Anansi, "I can't breathe."

Again the second and third threads were pulled and tightened around Anansi's middle. Anansi could hardly breathe they were so tight.

"I have to cut them, but if I do I'll miss the parties." Again the second and third threads were pulled. Hardly able to breathe, Anansi wheezed. "There will still be one party I can go to," he said as he cut the two threads.

"That's better," he said, rubbing his middle.

Suddenly the fourth and last thread was pulled.

"A party," said Anansi, with a large smile. "I'm going to a party."

The thread was pulled again.

"Ouch!" said Anansi. "That's getting tight, but I can't cut it otherwise I'll miss the party."

The thread was pulled again.

"Oh my," wheezed Anansi, "I can hardly breathe, but I'm not cutting this thread; I'll miss the party."

The thread was jerked again, but this time it snapped.

"No!" shouted Anansi. "How will I know where the party is? I'll miss it."

And that's how Anansi managed to miss four parties on the same night.

• • •

ANANSI INVITES TURTLE TO TEA

Anansi sat a little way from the river, enjoying the cool shade of his favorite tree.

"This is the life," he said, smiling.

He then noticed Turtle coming out of the river. Anansi's smile grew broader. "I have an idea," he said, mischievously.

Anansi took some food from his bag and placed it beside him on a brightly colored piece of cloth. He looked at Turtle and noticed small beads of sweat forming on Turtle's brow as he plodded. You see, turtles aren't built for speed on land; their little legs and heavy shells make them very slow. But they are fantastic swimmers and can stay under water for a long, long time.

Finally, Turtle reached Anansi and breathed a sigh of relief.

"Hello," Turtle said, puffing. "Hot today, isn't it?"

"Yes, it is," agreed Anansi.

Turtle licked his dry lips.

"Would you like some water?" asked Anansi, offering a gourd full of fresh, clean water.

"Thank you," replied Turtle, taking the gourd.

Anansi heard Turtle's stomach rumble.

"Sorry," said Turtle, looking a little embarrassed.

"Think nothing of it, my dear friend," replied Anansi. "I have some food here. Please join me."

"Thank you," replied Turtle, looking down at the food and licking his lips.

Suddenly a gust of wind whipped up the cloth and threw the food onto the ground. Anansi and Turtle watched as the cloth danced on the wind, then landed in a nearby bush.

"Turtle," said Anansi, wincing, "would you be kind enough to fetch that for me. I'm in terrible pain with my poor back."

"It's the least I can do," replied Turtle as he headed towards the bush.

Whilst Turtle went to fetch the cloth Anansi ate the food. As he popped the last piece into his mouth Turtle returned.

"You are a great friend," said Anansi. "Thank you."

Turtle looked around. "Have you eaten all the food?" he asked.

"I'm sorry," said Anansi, pretending to be ashamed. "I didn't realize I'd eaten it all. I was busy watching you."

Turtle's stomach rumbled again.

"No matter," said Anansi, putting his hand into his bag. "My wife cooked some kelewele last night and we had a little left over. She used the freshest plantains and just the right amount of ginger and chili. It's delicious. We can share that."

"Thank you," replied Turtle, licking his lips.

Anansi picked up the gourd and shook it. "Oh dear," he said, "the gourd is empty and I'm so thirsty. Would you be kind enough to fetch some more from the river for me? I'm in such pain with my poor back. I just can't bend down."

"Of course I can," said Turtle. "It's the least I can do.

As Anansi watched Turtle slowly walk to the edge of the river he popped a piece of kelewele into his mouth.

"Mmm," he said, eating another and another. By the time Turtle returned with the gourd full of water it was all gone.

Thank you," said Anansi, taking a large drink of cool water.

Turtle looked down and noticed Anansi had eaten all the kelewele.

"Well, my dear friend, it was so lovely to share my meal with you. Perhaps we should do it again and next time you can supply the food," said Anansi.

"But ..." said Turtle.

"No need to thank me," said Anansi, slowly getting up. "It was a pleasure to share my food with you."

"But ..."

"Perhaps tomorrow," said Anansi, placing his bag over his shoulder and wincing. "My poor back, it'll take me ages to walk home. But no matter, I have our lunch to look forward to. That'll take my mind off my poor back."

Turtle shook his head as he watched Anansi walk stiffly back to the village.

"What a lovely day," said Anansi to himself as he walked to Turtle's house. "I wonder what he'll serve. Perhaps plantains, maybe cassavas or, hopefully, yams."

When Anansi reached the edge of the river he noticed Turtle sunning himself on a large rock.

"Turtle, my friend," said Anansi, "I've looked forward to this all morning."

"So have I," replied Turtle. "I've set out a huge feast for us on my favorite spot."

Anansi looked around, confused. "Where?" he asked.

"Follow me," said Turtle, with a broad smile.

Anansi watched Turtle slip into the river and swim to the middle.

"Come on in," said Turtle, "the water's fresh and clear. This is the coolest place I could think of." Turtle disappeared under the gentle rippling waves of the river.

"Who does he think I am?" said Anansi, annoyed. "How can we eat under water?"

Turtle's head popped back up. "Anansi, come on! You'll not believe the feast I've prepared."

"But ..." said Anansi. His stomach gave a huge grumble. Placing his hand on his stomach, he said, "Perhaps I can hold my breath and eat at the same time."

Anansi placed his bag on the ground and stepped into the water.

"Brrr, that's cold," he said as the water lapped around his ankles. When Anansi reached the middle of the river he took a deep breath and dived.

Sure enough, on the bottom of the river Turtle had set

up a wonderful-looking feast. Anansi dived, but just as he reached the food his lungs began to burn. I need air, he thought.

He pointed upwards and swam back to the surface.

"I'll never get anything to eat at this rate," Anansi muttered angrily. "I'll have to take a bigger breath." So he breathed in deeply, held his nose and dived back to the bottom of the river.

As he sat on the bottom of the river and reached for a piece of food his lungs started to burn again. Anansi swam to the surface a second, a third and a fourth time. Finally, he gave up and swam back to the shore.

As he sat gasping for breath Turtle's head popped out of the water.

"Anansi, thank you so much for coming. I do hope you enjoyed it. Perhaps I should come to you next time."

"Turtle ..." said Anansi.

"No need to thank me, friend. It was a pleasure to share with you," replied Turtle, disappearing beneath the gentle ripples of the river.

• • •

HOW ANANSI, FLY AND ANT WON THE SUN

One morning the sun didn't come up. The next morning the sun didn't come up. After weeks of the sun not rising above the horizon Lion called a meeting with all the animals.

"This cannot go on," he roared. "Someone must visit the sun god and ask for the sun to rise again."

The animals looked around, waiting for someone else to step forward and volunteer. Slowly, Eagle stepped forward. "I'll go," he said. "I'm sure I can soar high enough."

Lion nodded his approval and all the animals watched in the moonlight as Eagle flew higher and higher. Soon Eagle was just a small dot against the moon. As Eagle continued to climb his wings became very tired.

"I'm just not strong enough," Eagle said. "I need a strong breeze to lift me higher."

Eagle continued to climb; he didn't want to fail Lion. "It's no good," puffed Eagle, "I just cannot get high enough."

When he returned he stood in front of Lion hanging his head in shame. "I'm sorry, I was sure I'd be strong enough, but I just can't reach the sun god."

"At least you tried," said Lion. "Who else is ready to try and wake the sun god?" he asked the other animals.

"I'll try," said Monkey. "I can swing from tree to tree to the top of the mountain."

Lion nodded and Monkey disappeared into the forest. Sometime later Monkey returned holding her head in shame.

"I'm sorry," she said. "I couldn't make it to the summit of the mountain. The trees didn't go all the way to the top."

"At least you tried," said Lion. "Who else is ready to try and wake the sun god?" he asked.

Everyone looked around waiting for someone else to volunteer. If Eagle wasn't strong enough to fly to where the sun god lived, and Monkey couldn't either, how could they?

Anansi had been watching this from his tree and he decided this would be a good time to show the animals just how clever he was. So he slipped down from his tree and walked up to Lion.

"I'll go," he said. "I have a clever plan. But I'll need to take someone with me."

"Who do you need?" asked Lion.

All the animals held their breath and hoped he wouldn't pick them.

"For my plan to work I'll need Ant and Fly," Anansi said.

"Are you sure?" asked Lion. "They're not the strongest in the jungle."

"I'm sure," replied Anansi.

"Ant and Fly, come here," roared Lion. Slowly, Ant and Fly came forward and stood in front of Lion. "Are you willing to help Anansi?" he asked them.

Ant swallowed hard because he didn't want to upset Lion. "I am," he said quietly.

"Good," said Lion. "Fly, are you willing to help Anansi?"

Fly buzzed quietly, wishing she had the courage to say no to Lion. "Yezzz," she replied.

Just then a great gust of wind blew down from the mountain.

"Fly," said Anansi, "quickly take this silken thread and, with the aid of the wind, fly as high as you can. When you reach the clouds, attach it firmly."

Fly took the thread and flew upwards. She beat her little wings as hard as she could. Eventually she reached the clouds and attached the silken thread. Then she grabbed it and slid back down to earth.

"It izz done," she said, gasping.

Anansi began to climb the silken thread and as he did he left another attached to the ground. When he reached the clouds he fastened it firmly and came back down. He repeated this four more times, then spun a web that looked like a ladder. Once the ladder was finished he said, "Ant, climb up and cut a hole in the clouds, so we can climb through."

So up Ant climbed and cut a hole in the clouds. Anansi, seeing the hole, climbed and Fly followed.

Soon Ant, Fly and Anansi were standing at the edge of

the hole looking in wonder at the world of the sun god.

"What now?" Ant asked Anansi.

But before Anansi could reply a huge tent appeared in front of them and out strode the sun god.

"What do you want?" his voice boomed.

Anansi stepped forward. "We need the sun," he told the sun god.

The sun god laughed. "Why should I let you use my sun?"

"Without it we cannot see to eat, we cannot see to drink and we cannot see to help one another," replied Anansi.

The sun god laughed again. "I'll let you have the sun back if you can complete three tasks. If you don't succeed, then you'll never see the sun again."

"What are they?" asked Anansi. "I'm sure we can complete them."

The sun god scratched his chin as he pondered what task to set. Finally, he said, "See that field of grass over there?"

Ant, Fly and Anansi looked, but they couldn't see a field of grass.

"Look harder," said the sun god. Suddenly the largest field of grass Ant, Fly or Anansi had ever seen appeared in front of them. "Cut every blade of grass in that field by morning and you'll have completed the first task."

Fly gasped. "We'll ..."

But Anansi didn't let her finish. "That's easy," he said confidently.

The sun god laughed. "I'll be back tomorrow and then we'll see." He turned around and strode back to his huge tent.

"How will we ever cut all that grass?" asked Fly.

"We won't," Anansi replied, "but Ant and all of his family will be able to do it."

Ant nodded and scurried down the ladder to fetch his family.

As Fly and Anansi waited, Anansi said to Fly, "Sneak into the sun god's tent, hide, and see if you can discover what the second task is going to be."

Fly nodded and flew off to see if she could find out what the next task would be.

Soon Ant returned with his family. They worked all night chomping at the blades of grass and cutting them. They'd just finished when Fly came out of the tent.

"Quickly, the sun god is coming!" she told Anansi.

"Let him come," said Anansi. "Ant and his family have cut all the grass." Anansi then asked, "What's the next task?"

"We're to eat all the fruit on the fruit treezz in the field," said Fly.

"But there are no fruit trees," said Anansi. "Are you sure that's what you heard?"

"Yezz," replied Fly.

As Ant's family disappeared down the ladder the sun god came out of his tent.

He laughed, but not as much as he did the day before. "I see you've cut the grass. Well done. But I'm sure you'll never complete the second task."

"What is the task?" asked Anansi.

"You need to eat all the fruit on all the trees in the field," the sun god said.

"But there are no trees," said Anansi, confused.

"Look a little harder," the sun god told them.

As Ant, Fly and Anansi stared at the huge field, fruit trees began to grow. Soon they were full of the largest, juiciest fruit you've ever seen.

Ant gasped, "How...?"

But Anansi didn't let him finish. "That's easy," he said confidently.

The sun god laughed. "I'll be back tomorrow and then we'll see." He turned around and strode back to his huge tent.

"How will we ever eat all that fruit?" asked Ant.

"We won't," Anansi told him. "Fly and her family will."

Fly nodded and went down the web ladder to fetch her family.

As they waited Anansi said to Ant, "I need you to creep into the sun god's tent and discover what the next task is."

So Ant scurried away, slipped into the tent and hid.

Soon Fly and her family returned and began to eat the delicious juicy fruit. They ate and ate and they ate. Just as the next day arrived they swallowed the last morsel of fruit and disappeared down the ladder.

Anansi and Fly hadn't seen Ant come back.

"Choose the small grey square box," said Ant, making Anansi and Fly jump.

"Pardon?" asked Anansi.

"The sun god is going to give you a choice of boxes.

Take the small grey box."

"Are you sure?" asked Anansi.

"Yes," replied Ant.

Just then the sun god came out of the tent stretching and yawning. "What a wonderful night's sleep," he said as he walked towards them. But he scowled when he noticed all the fruit had been eaten. "It would seem you've completed the second task," he said.

"It was easy," boasted Anansi. "I hope the next one is a little more difficult."

"I've decided to be kind to you," said the sun god, with a smile. "For the third task all you have to do is choose the correct box."

"That sounds simple enough," said Anansi. "I'm sure ..." but he didn't have time to finish his sentence when a box appeared, floating above his head. Then another appeared, and another and another until there were 101 boxes hovering in the air. They were all different colors, shapes and sizes.

"Just pick the correct one and you've completed all three tasks," said the sun god, with a smile.

Anansi pointed at a large yellow box. "Not that one," he said. He pointed at another. "Not that one either." He continued to point at boxes until there was only one box left. "We'll take that one," he said, gently grasping a small grey square box.

"Are you sure?" asked the sun god, looking slightly annoyed.

"I am," replied Anansi.

"Well, open it," the sun god told Anansi.

"I'm so sure I've picked the right one I'm going to give that honor to King Lion," said Anansi.

Anansi, Ant and Fly climbed down the ladder and found the animals waiting for them.

"The sun's not come up," roared Lion. "You've obviously failed, Anansi. We need someone else to talk to the sun god."

"Before you send someone else," said Anansi, "open this box."

"What's inside?" Lion asked.

"We don't know," said Ant.

Lion carefully took the box and placed it on the ground.

"Is this a trick, Anansi?" asked Lion.

"No, Lion, please open it," said Anansi.

Lion sighed and slowly opened the box. He stood back, but nothing happened. So Lion tapped the box with his foot. Suddenly a rooster jumped out and ruffled his feathers.

"What good is a rooster?" roared Lion angrily.

The rooster ruffled his feathers again and threw back his head. "Cock-a-doodle-do!" he crowed.

The animals held their breath and the rooster crowed again. "Cock-a-doodle-do!"

The animals gasped. The animals cheered. The sun was up!

• • •

ANANSI AND THE TALKING MELON

It was hot and Anansi had climbed into a tree to keep cool in its branches. As he looked down he noticed Elephant working in his field, tending the juicy, ripe melons he'd spent months growing.

Anansi licked his lips. "Mmm, they look good," he said. "I wonder if Elephant would miss one?"

As Anansi continued to watch it became hotter and hotter and the sun climbed higher into the sky. Elephant looked up and wiped the sweat from his brow. "Phew, I must get a drink and something to eat," he said.

Anansi watched Elephant put down his hoe, walk out of the field and along the road to his house.

"I'll just treat myself to one melon whilst Elephant is gone," said Anansi to himself. "Just one small melon; he'll never notice."

So Anansi climbed down the tree, opened the gate and went into Elephant's melon field. He looked around to make sure no one had seen him and picked up a melon; but Anansi became greedy.

"I know I said just one small melon, but this one is too small." Anansi put down the small melon and picked up another. But he put that down too when he noticed a huge melon growing by the wooden fence that surrounded Elephant's melon field. Anansi tried to pick it up, but it was so big he couldn't.

"This one will do," said Anansi, his mouth beginning to water.

He looked at the melon, then scratched his head. "How am I going to get it open?" he asked himself.

Anansi looked around, then smiled. "I know, I'll break one of the thorns from that thorn bush," he said.

Soon Anansi had made a hole in the side of the melon and had crawled inside. He ate and he ate and he ate.

"This is the best melon I've ever tasted," Anansi said, between large bites of melon.

After a while Anansi had eaten more than his fill and he sat back and placed his hand on his now very round stomach. "I couldn't eat another mouthful," he said.

Suddenly Anansi heard the creak of the gate as Elephant returned.

"I'd better get out of here," Anansi said quietly. But when Anansi tried to fit through the hole he couldn't get out. He tried this way and that, but however hard he tried, he couldn't squeeze back out of the melon.

"Oh bother!" said Anansi. "What am I going to do?"

"Who said that?" Anansi heard Elephant ask.

Anansi didn't move. He didn't breathe. Then he smiled. "I can have some fun here," he said, "and get myself out of this melon at the same time."

Anansi felt the melon move as Elephant picked it up.

"Put me down at once," shouted Anansi. "Don't you know it's rude to pick someone up without asking?"

Elephant dropped the melon. "Who said that?" he asked.

"Ouch, be careful," said Anansi, trying not to laugh.

"Where are you?" Elephant asked.

"By your feet," replied Anansi. "I'm lying where you so rudely dropped me."

"Don't be daft. Melons can't talk," said Elephant.

"If melons can't talk, then who's the daft one?" said Anansi, trying even harder not to laugh.

"Well I never!" said Elephant. "I've never met a talking melon before. I didn't know you could talk."

"You didn't ask," replied Anansi.

"I'm going to take you to the chief," said Elephant, as he carefully picked up the melon.

As Elephant walked along the road Anansi said, "You take care with me. You don't want to drop me."

"I'll be careful," replied Elephant.

After a while Elephant bumped into Rhino.

"Where are you going in such a hurry with that melon?" Rhino asked.

"I'm going to show it to the chief," replied Elephant. "It's a very special melon."

"It doesn't look special to me," said Rhino.

"What would you know?" said Anansi, still trapped inside the melon.

"Oh my!" said Rhino, shocked the melon was talking to him. "I can see why you want to show it to the chief."

"Who would believe I could grow a talking melon?" said Elephant.

"Can I come with you?" asked Rhino. "I want to see the chief's face when he hears the melon talk."

"Please join us," said Anansi.

"Thank you, melon," replied Rhino.

So Elephant and Rhino walked along the road with Elephant carefully holding the melon.

Soon they bumped into Warthog, who asked, "Where are you both going in such a hurry with that huge melon?"

"We're going to see the chief," Rhino told him. "Elephant grew a talking melon."

"I don't believe it," said Warthog, looking closely at the melon.

"Who are you looking at?" asked Anansi.

"Who said that?" asked Warthog.

"The melon," said Elephant.

"Really?" asked Warthog.

"Yes," said Anansi, trying very hard not to laugh.

"Well, I've never heard of a talking melon," said Warthog. "I can understand why you want to show it to the chief. Can I come?"

"Please join us," said Anansi. "The more who see the chief's face the better."

So Elephant, Rhino and Warthog walked along the road with Elephant carefully carrying the melon.

As they walked they bumped into Goat, Turtle and Bushbuck, who all agreed the chief would want to see a talking melon. So they joined Elephant, Rhino and

Warthog and walked to the village.

When they finally reached the village Anansi said, "I think you'll find the chief in his hut."

"I'm sure you're right, melon," agreed Elephant. "We'll go there first."

When they arrived at the chief's hut Elephant knocked gently on the door and waited. No one answered.

"Knock again," Rhino told Elephant. So Elephant knocked again, a little harder this time. There was still no answer.

"Knock again," said Warthog. So Elephant knocked again a little harder still.

The animals heard movement inside and the door opened.

"What's the meaning of this?" asked the chief, coming out into the bright light. "Can't you just leave me alone? I was enjoying a wonderful nap."

"We have something special to show you," said Rhino, pushing Elephant forward.

"Couldn't it wait?" asked the chief.

"We were sure you'd want to see this," said Warthog.

"Elephant, go on, show him," said Goat.

"Come on, Elephant, show me then," said the chief, becoming impatient. "I'd like to go back and continue my nap."

"I've grown a talking melon," said Elephant, holding the melon out for the chief to see.

"You've grown a talking melon?" asked the chief. "You really want me to believe you've grown a talking melon?"

"It really does talk," replied Elephant, holding it out closer to the chief for him to see.

"Well ..." said the chief, prodding the melon with his finger, "talk."

But Anansi didn't say a word.

Elephant shook the melon. "Talk to the chief," he ordered the melon.

Everyone waited, but Anansi kept quiet.

"I'm waiting, melon," the chief said. "You don't have to be shy, just a few words."

Again Anansi didn't say a word.

Elephant shook the melon again. "Please, melon, talk to the chief," he pleaded.

Anansi didn't say a word.

"I'm getting angry now," said the chief, his face becoming red. "Elephant, is this a joke?"

"No, oh no, chief," replied Elephant, a little scared.

"Then make the melon talk," ordered the chief.

Elephant shook the melon. "Melon, talk. I order you to talk to the chief."

Still Anansi didn't say a word.

"Do you think I'm stupid?" shouted the chief, who was now very angry.

The animals had never seen the chief as angry. "Stop wasting my time!" shouted the chief. "I'm going back to bed."

He grabbed the melon from Elephant and threw it as hard as he could. The melon flew through the air with Anansi inside. Finally, it crashed into the trunk of a banana tree and broke into lots of tiny pieces.

"At last I'm free," said Anansi. He shook off the melon seeds that covered him from head to toe.

Just then he saw Elephant stomping in his direction looking very angry.

I'd better hide in this banana tree," Anansi said. "He may wonder why I'm covered in melon seeds."

Anansi quickly climbed the tree and as he hid among the lovely ripe bananas Elephant walked under its leaves.

"That's it," said Elephant, "I'm never going to grow melons again."

"I wouldn't either," said Anansi, trying not to laugh. "Us bananas are much easier to grow and much less trouble."

• • •

ANANSI AND THE MOSS-COVERED ROCK

Anansi had decided that rather than working he would go for a walk in the jungle.

"This is nice," he said. "Everyone else is busy and I have the jungle to myself."

Suddenly he tripped and fell. "Ouch!" he said. "What was that?"

Anansi got up and rubbed one of his many knees. "That'll be bruised in the morning," he said, wincing.

He looked down. "That is a strange-looking rock," he said. "It's covered ..." But before he had time to finish his sentence he was asleep, curled around the rock snoring and dreaming of sleeping under his favorite tree.

Sometime later Anansi woke up. "Where am I?" he asked, confused. "I remember," he said, getting up and stretching. "I was having a lovely walk when I tripped over that rock."

Anansi looked down at the rock. "It is a strange-looking rock," he said. "I wonder ..." Again, before he had time to finish his sentence he was asleep, curled around the rock and dreaming of eating a huge feast of cassavas.

A little later Anansi woke up. "Where am I?" he asked,

confused. "I remember," he said. Then he smiled. "And I think I've been lucky enough to discover a magic rock."

Anansi smiled and looked down at the rock. "I'm going to have fun with you."

The next day Anansi went to see Goat.

"Hello," said Anansi, finding Goat outside her house washing fresh fruits and vegetables. "Hot today, isn't it?"

"It is," replied Goat. "Far too hot to be working."

"You're so right," agreed Anansi. "Why don't we go for a walk in the cool cover of the jungle?"

"I have so much to do," said Goat. "I don't really have time."

"You work too hard," Anansi told Goat. "Just a short walk in the cool shade of the jungle will do you the world of good."

"Anansi, I think you're right," said Goat. "Let's go for that walk."

So Goat and Anansi walked into the jungle, chatting. Soon they came to the place where Anansi had fallen over the moss-covered rock.

"Ouch!" shouted Anansi, pretending to trip over the rock.

"Are you all right?" asked Goat.

"I think so," said Anansi. Wincing, he pulled himself up and rubbed one of his many knees. "I wonder what made me trip up?" he asked.

Goat looked down and saw the moss-covered rock. "What a strange-looking rock," she said, "I think you tripped ..." But before she had time to finish she was fast asleep, curled around the rock and dreaming about paddling in the cool waters of the nearby river.

Suddenly Anansi heard a small rustle. "Who's there?" he asked. He listened again, but didn't hear anything. Must be my imagination, he thought.

Anansi looked down at Goat. "Sleep well, Goat," he said. Anansi then hurried back to Goat's house to collect the fruit and vegetables she'd left drying in the sun.

The next day, when Anansi finally managed to drag himself out of bed, he said, "I think I'll visit Zebra today." So Anansi walked to Zebra's house.

"Hello," said Anansi, finding Zebra outside his house preparing lunch. "Hot today, isn't it?"

"Far too hot to be working," replied Zebra.

"You work too hard," Anansi told Zebra. "Why don't you join me for a short walk in the cool shade of the jungle? It'll do you the world of good."

"Anansi, I think I will," said Zebra. "Thank you for your kind invitation."

So Zebra and Anansi walked into the jungle, chatting. Soon they came to the place where Anansi had fallen over the moss-covered rock.

Again Anansi pretended to trip over the rock.

"Are you all right?" asked Zebra, concerned.

"I think so," Anansi replied. "I wonder what I tripped over?" he asked.

Zebra looked down and saw the moss-covered rock. "What a strange-looking rock," he said. "I think you tripped ..." But before he had time to finish he was curled around the moss-covered rock fast asleep and dreaming about galloping through lush green grass.

"Sleep well, Zebra," said Anansi.

Anansi heard a small rustle. "Who's there?" he asked. He listened again, but he didn't hear anything. Must have been my imagination, he thought.

Anansi hurried back to Zebra's house to collect the food he'd been preparing for lunch.

The next day when Anansi finally managed to drag himself out of bed it was lunchtime and his stomach was grumbling. "I think I'll visit Warthog today," he said to himself as he stretched.

So he walked to Warthog's house.

"Hello," said Anansi, finding Warthog outside her house stirring a large pot of delicious-smelling food. "Hot today, isn't it?"

"It is," agreed Warthog. "Far too hot to be cooking."

"You work too hard," Anansi said. "Why don't you join me for a short walk in the cool shade of the jungle? It'll do you the world of good."

"I think I will," said Warthog.

Soon Warthog and Anansi were walking in the jungle, chatting. After a while they came to the place where Anansi had discovered the moss-covered rock.

"Ouch!" said Anansi, pretending to trip over the rock.

"Are you hurt?" asked Warthog.

"I'm fine, thank you," Anansi replied. "But I wonder what I tripped over? I didn't see anything. Did you?" he asked.

Warthog looked down and saw the moss-covered rock.

What a strange-looking rock," she said. "I think you tripped ..." But before she had time to finish she was asleep, curled around the rock, dreaming about walking in the jungle.

"Sleep well, Warthog," said Anansi, smiling.

Anansi heard a small rustle. "Who's there?" he asked. He listened, but didn't hear anything. "Just my imagination," he told himself, but he was wrong.

As Anansi hurried back to Warthog's house to collect the food she'd been cooking he didn't hear a voice whisper, "I think Anansi needs to learn a lesson."

The next day, just as Anansi came out of his hut, who should wander by but Bushbuck?

"Good morning," she said. "Far too hot to be working."

"It is," agreed Anansi.

"I'm going for a walk in the jungle," Bushbuck told Anansi. "Would you like to join me?"

Anansi smiled. "I'd love to," he said. "I can show you my favorite place in the jungle if you'd like to see it."

"That would be lovely," said Bushbuck.

Soon Anansi and Bushbuck came to the place where the moss-covered rock was. As he had done with Goat, Zebra and Warthog, Anansi pretended to trip.

"Ouch," he said, "that's another knee bruised. I wonder what I tripped over?"

Bushbuck looked around. "I can't see anything," she said. "I suppose having as many feet as you do tripping over is easy."

"No, no," replied Anansi. "I never trip over my feet. I must have tripped over something."

Bushbuck pretended to look. "I really can't see anything," she said.

"That rock," said Anansi.

"What rock?" asked Bushbuck, looking around.

"Don't you see it?" asked Anansi. "Just there. That rock."

Bushbuck shook her head. "I'm sorry, Anansi, but I don't see anything that could have tripped you up."

"There," shouted Anansi, pointing. "That strange-looking rock just ..." Before he could finish Anansi was fast asleep, curled around the moss-covered rock, dreaming about all the food he had at home.

"Sleep well, Anansi," said Bushbuck, as she went to find Goat, Zebra and Warthog to tell them how Anansi had tricked them and to collect the food he'd taken.

• • •

WHY ANANSI HAS THIN, LONG LEGS

One warm, sunny afternoon Anansi was taking a stroll around the village enjoying being lazy and not working. Just as he walked passed Goat's house his stomach gave a huge grumble.

Goat looked up from the fresh cassava she was washing and smiled.

"Excuse me," said Anansi, "my stomach is telling me it's empty."

"You are more than welcome to join me once my meal is cooked," said Goat.

"That's very kind of you," said Anansi, "but I've got to be somewhere."

"That's a shame," replied Goat.

Anansi thought for a moment, as he disliked missing out on a free meal.

"I have a clever idea," said Anansi. "I'll tie one of my silken threads to one of my ankles and give the other end to you. When the meal is ready, tug on the thread and I'll join you."

"You are clever," said Goat.

So Anansi spun a long silken thread and tied one end

around his first ankle and gave the other end to Goat.

"See you later," said Anansi, waving.

As he continued on his way Anansi licked his lips. "Cassava is perhaps my most favorite food," he said. "Especially free cassava."

Anansi then passed Rabbit's house.

"Hello, Rabbit," Anansi shouted, stopping at the gate.

Rabbit peeked around the open door and came out. "Hello, Anansi," she said, "how are you?"

"I'm well," replied Anansi. "What are you up to?"

"Washing some plantains for my evening meal," replied Rabbit.

Anansi's stomach gave the hugest growl you've ever heard.

"Well, excuse me," said Anansi. "My stomach is telling me it's empty."

"You are more than welcome to join me," said Rabbit.

"That's very kind of you," said Anansi, "but I've got somewhere to be."

"That's a shame," replied Rabbit. "It would have been nice to have your company."

Anansi pretended to think for a moment. "I have a clever idea," he said. "I'll tie one of my silken threads to one of my legs and give the other end to you. When the meal is ready, tug on the thread and I'll join you. That way neither of us is eating alone."

"What a clever idea," said Rabbit.

So Anansi spun the longest silken thread you've ever seen and tied one end around his second ankle and gave the other end to Rabbit.

"See you later," said Anansi, waving.

"I look forward to it," said Rabbit, going back indoors.

Anansi continued to walk and as he did the sun slowly began to set.

"What a beautiful sight," sighed Anansi.

"It is a glorious evening, isn't it?" said Hyena, who was outside chopping food. "I just love the way the sun paints the sky with so many colors."

"It is," replied Anansi. Just then his stomach gave a huge rumble. "Well, excuse me," said Anansi holding his stomach. "It appears I'm hungry."

"I have plenty of food," said Hyena. "You are more than welcome to join me."

"That is a very kind offer," said Anansi "but I have somewhere to be."

"That is a pity," replied Hyena.

Anansi pretended to think for a moment. "I have a clever idea," said Anansi. "I'll tie a silken thread to one of my legs and give the other end to you. When the meal is ready, tug on the thread and I'll join you."

"You are clever," said Hyena.

So Anansi spun a silken thread and tied one end around his third ankle and gave the other end to Hyena.

"I look forward to sharing a meal with you," said Anansi. "See you later."

"Yes, see you later," replied Hyena, continuing to prepare the food.

As Anansi continued to walk and enjoy the evening air

he bumped into Zebra, then Warthog, then Rhino, then Elephant and finally Bushbuck. All were busy cooking themselves a meal. Each time he was talking to one of them Anansi's stomach gave a great big grumble. If I didn't know better I'd say Anansi had taught his stomach to grumble just at the right time.

But that's not possible. Is it?

Now Zebra, Warthog, Rhino, Elephant and Bushbuck are polite animals so they all asked Anansi if he'd like to join them. Each time he was asked Anansi pretended to think about it and suggest he would tie a silken thread around one of his ankles.

"That is clever," said Zebra.

"I would never have come up with that idea," said Warthog.

"You do amaze me sometimes," said Rhino. "How you come up with all these clever ideas."

By the time Anansi had finished his walk he had eight offers of a free meal and eight silken threads attached to each of his eight ankles.

Anansi rubbed his stomach and licked his lips. "I wonder who I'll be eating with tonight?" he asked. "And I wonder what glorious meal I'll be eating? I can't wait."

Anansi settled down under his favorite tree and watched the moon and the stars come out. Suddenly Anansi felt a silken thread tighten around one of his ankles.

"I wonder who has the other end?" Anansi asked himself.

Then the second silken thread started to tighten around

another ankle.

"Oh, two meals are ready. If only I could remember who has the other end. I could then choose my favorite meal."

As he was trying to decide which silken thread to follow another began to tighten around an ankle, then another and another. Soon all eight threads were being pulled.

"Who to choose?" said Anansi. "I just don't know."

All the threads were pulled again and again and they became tighter and tighter.

"This isn't nice," said Anansi. "These threads are becoming far too tight. They're stopping the blood going into my feet."

Suddenly all eight threads were pulled and pulled and pulled. Anansi's eight legs were pulled in all directions and they became a little longer and a little thinner.

"Please stop!" he cried out, trying to cut the threads.

But Goat, Rabbit, Hyena, Zebra, Warthog, Rhino, Elephant and Bushbuck continued to pull on the threads.

"Please stop!" Anansi shouted, as his legs become a little longer still and a little thinner.

Suddenly all the threads stopped being pulled and Anansi fell to the ground. He quickly cut the threads.

"Now I can't go anywhere," sulked Anansi. "My legs hurt too much."

Then he thought for a moment. "It's strange how all the threads were pulled at once. It was as if everyone knew." Anansi shook his head. "No, that's impossible. How could they?"

· · ·

ANANSI AND THE FIELD OF CORN

Each morning as Anansi watched Monkey swing through the trees he muttered, "I wonder where she's going?"

Finally, Anansi decided to find out where Monkey went each morning in such a hurry.

"I'll never keep up with her," Anansi said. Anansi thought for a while, then smiled. "Anansi, you're such a clever fellow."

The next day when Anansi saw Monkey he called out, "Morning, Monkey, how are you today?"

Monkey stopped for a moment and replied, "I'm well, Anansi, how are you?"

Anansi shook his head. "Sorry, Monkey, I can't hear you. Can you come down from the trees?"

Monkey came down and as they chatted Anansi leant forward. "You have a leaf stuck in your tail. Let me remove it for you."

As Anansi pretended to remove the leaf he attached an invisible silken thread to Monkey's tail.

"There you go," he said. "Well, I must get on. Lovely to chat to you."

"And you," replied Monkey, who returned to the trees

and went on her way.

"Now all I have to do is wait until the thread stops moving and I can follow it," Anansi said, smiling.

Soon the thread stopped moving and Anansi started to follow it through the trees. It wove in and out of the branches and far away from the village.

Anansi became excited. "She must be keeping a very big secret if she travels this far."

Finally, Anansi reached the end of the thread and, to his surprise, there was a field full of golden ripe corn. In the field Monkey was busy gathering some of her harvest.

"So this is where Monkey comes each morning," Anansi said. "This is a field to be proud of." Then Anansi became greedy. "I will make this field mine," he said, "but how?"

Anansi returned home and sat under the shade of his favorite tree. He thought and thought and thought. "How can I make Monkey's field mine?" he asked himself. Finally, he smiled. "Anansi, you're a clever fellow."

The next day Anansi collected together some broken pots and a machete. He started to cut a path to Monkey's field. "Just a piece of pot here," said Anansi, dropping some pot on the ground, "and another here. Then it'll look as if I've used this path for years."

By the time the sun was high in the sky Anansi reached the field full of golden ripe corn.

"Phew, that was hard work!" Anansi said, wiping the beads of sweat from his brow. "But it was worth it. Just look at this beautiful field of delicious corn."

Anansi got to work collecting some of the corn and

placed it in a bag. As he finished Monkey appeared from the trees.

"What are you doing?" shouted Monkey angrily. "This is my field."

"How can it be your field?" asked Anansi. "There's only one path to this field and it starts at my front door."

"This is my field," Monkey insisted.

"No, it is mine," said Anansi, trying to hide a smile.

"We'll go and see the chief and ask him what he thinks," said Monkey, looking very red in the face. She turned around and disappeared into the forest.

Anansi smiled, closed the bag, and walked along the path. When he reached his house Monkey and the chief were standing by his front door.

The chief looked very stern, "I understand you've been stealing from Monkey's field, Anansi. Is this true?"

"It is not," said Anansi, firmly. "Did you see me walk along this path?" he asked.

"I did," replied the chief.

"Then let me take you to the field," said Anansi. "I'll prove it's my field."

Monkey started to shout, but the chief held up his hand. "Anansi, this had better not be one of your tricks."

"It isn't," replied Anansi. "I just want to prove the field is mine."

"Then show the way," said the chief.

As they walked the chief noticed the broken pieces of pot. "So you've used this path for many years?" he asked.

"I have," replied Anansi.

The chief nodded.

Soon they reached the edge of the field.

"Here's my field," said Anansi.

"It's MINE!" shouted Monkey angrily.

"There's only one path," said Anansi, "and it comes from my house. That proves it's mine."

"Are you sure there is only one path?" asked the chief.

"Wise Chief," Anansi said. "Walk around the field to see if you can see another."

So the chief, Anansi and Monkey walked around the edges of the field and, just as Anansi had said, there was only one path.

The chief sighed. "Sorry, Monkey, I can only see one path and it starts at Anansi's house. If there were two paths then I would say share, but it appears this is Anansi's field."

Monkey let out a scream of frustration, leapt into a nearby tree and disappeared into the jungle.

"I hope you've not tricked me," the chief warned Anansi.

A few days later as Anansi collected some of the golden ripe corn he didn't notice the large grey clouds filling the sky. He didn't notice as the wind became colder. Just as Anansi put the last piece of corn into his bag he looked up.

"Oh my," he said, "I'll have to hurry."

As Anansi started to run along the path the first few rain drops began to fall. "I really must hurry," Anansi said.

But he'd left it too late. Soon the rain was falling in the largest drops you've ever seen. The wind was ripping at the bag on his shoulder and the thunder and lightning were crashing around his ears.

In his hurry to get home the bag fell open and the corn dropped to the ground.

"Oh bother!" Anansi said. "I'll come back later. This storm is too fierce for me."

By the time Anansi reached home the storm was tearing the leaves from the trees and ripping up fences. Everyone was hiding in their homes, hoping it would soon pass. Well, that was everyone apart from Crow, who had seen Anansi drop the corn.

"Why, Anansi, thank you," said Crow, with a smile. "That corn does look nice and only a fool would leave corn in the middle of a path."

Crow flew down from his tree, stood over the corn, curved his wings out and covered his head. Here he stayed all night, protected under his waterproof wings.

When the sun came up and dried his feathers Crow shook himself and started to pick up the corn. As he picked up the last piece he heard Anansi shouting, "That's my corn! Put it down."

"Your corn, you say," replied Crow. "Only a fool would leave corn out in a storm."

"It's mine, I tell you!" shouted Anansi.

"So you are a fool," said Crow. "I have an idea. Let's ask the chief, to see what he thinks."

Anansi thought for a moment, then said to himself so Crow couldn't hear, "I don't want the chief to think I'm a fool. It's only a small amount of corn."

"Shall we go?" asked Crow.

"No, I wouldn't want to bother the chief," replied Anansi. "You saved the corn from the storm, so you should be rewarded. Take the corn. I have plenty more where that came from."

"That's kind of you," said Crow, with a smile.

"You're welcome," said Anansi, a little annoyed.

As Anansi walked along the path he began to think about the delicious meals the corn would be turned into. But when he arrived at the edge of the field he couldn't believe his eyes.

The storm had ripped thought the field and destroyed the ripe golden corn. There was nothing left.

"No!" he screamed. "This isn't fair. What have I done to deserve this?"

• • •

ANANSI AND THE TUG OF WAR

It was a warm, sunny day and Anansi was resting in his normal place in the shade of his favorite tree, watching the river lap upon the shore.

"This is the life," he said. "No work, but plenty of rest."

Suddenly Anansi heard Elephant crashing through the forest. He watched Elephant as he waded into the river and took a long, long drink.

"Lovely," said Elephant as the last drop of cool, clean water trickled down the back of his throat.

"Hello, Elephant," said Anansi, but Elephant didn't hear Anansi. He was busy filling his trunk with more cool, clean water.

"Hello, Elephant," Anansi repeated, but Elephant still didn't hear him.

"I need a sit down," Elephant said, shaking his trunk dry. Not really looking where he was going, Elephant ambled over to Anansi's favorite spot and sat down, almost squashing Anansi.

"Watch out!" shouted Anansi, jumping out of the way.

Elephant looked around, surprised. "Sorry, Anansi, I didn't see you there."

"Well, take more care," said Anansi, annoyed.

"Don't make such a fuss," said Elephant. "How am I supposed to see such a small weak animal? It should be you that takes care to keep out of my way."

"Weak, am I?" shouted Anansi. "How dare you! I'm not weak."

Elephant snorted with laughter.

"I'll show you," said Anansi. "I challenge to you a game of tug of war."

"Don't be daft," Elephant said, between snorts of laughter. "I can easily beat you."

"Are you sure?" asked Anansi.

"Of course I am," replied Elephant. "And to prove I'm stronger than you, just say where and when and we'll have that tug of war."

"On the edge of the village, near the watering hole," replied Anansi. "Just after the sun has come up."

Once Elephant had stopped laughing he said, "See you then, Anansi."

Elephant got up and walked back into the jungle. As Anansi watched Elephant leave he said, "How on earth am I going to beat Elephant at a game of tug of war?"

Anansi thought and thought and finally he came up with an idea. He smiled and said, "Anansi, you are such a clever fellow."

To put his plan into action Anansi went to find Hippo. It didn't take long because Hippo was in his favorite place, resting at the edge of the river among the reeds.

"Hello, Hippo," said Anansi. "How funny to see you

here. Elephant and I were just talking about you."

"You were?" asked Hippo, lazily.

"Yes," replied Anansi. "We were arguing about who was stronger. Elephant agreed with me that I am stronger than you, but not as strong as he is."

Hippo roared with laughter. "Anansi, how you like to boast. There is no way you're stronger than me."

"I am," replied Anansi. "Even Elephant agrees."

"Well, you are both wrong," said Hippo.

"I'll prove it to you," said Anansi. "I challenge you to a game of tug of war."

"Don't be daft," Hippo said, between snorts of laughter. "I can easily beat you."

"Are you sure about that?" asked Anansi.

"Of course I am," replied Hippo. "To prove it, I accept your challenge. Just say where and when and we'll have this tug of war."

"On the edge of the river, beneath my favorite tree," replied Anansi. "Let's say just after the sun has come up."

Once Hippo had stopped laughing he said, "I'll see you then, Anansi."

The next morning Anansi was waiting for Elephant by the watering hole holding a very long piece of thick rope.

"Good morning," said Elephant. "Are you sure you want to do this?"

"Of course I am," said Anansi. "I've even brought this thick, strong rope I have."

"As long as you're sure," replied Elephant, smiling.

"You take this end and I'll take the other," Anansi told

Elephant, holding out the rope.

Elephant took the end of the long, thick rope and wound it around his trunk.

"When you feel a tug on the rope, start to pull," Anansi told Elephant.

Elephant nodded as Anansi took the other end of the rope.

"Remember, when you feel the tug on the rope, start to pull," said Anansi as he walked away from Elephant down to his favorite tree by the river.

As Anansi reached the tree he saw Hippo coming out of the river.

"Good morning," said Hippo. "Are you sure you want to do this?"

"Of course I am," said Anansi. "I've even brought this thick, strong rope."

"As long as you're sure," replied Hippo, smiling.

"Now you take this end and I'll take the other," Anansi told Hippo, holding out the rope. "Wait there whilst I go and grab the other end."

Hippo took the rope between his large flat teeth and nodded.

"Remember, when you feel the tug on the rope, start to pull," said Anansi as he walked away from Hippo.

When Anansi reached the middle of the rope he gave it a tug. Elephant felt the tug and began to pull. Hippo felt the tug and began to pull. Anansi stood back and watched the rope move back and forth between Hippo and Elephant.

"I do enjoy playing tricks," said Anansi, with a huge

smile.

Elephant wasn't going to be beaten by Anansi, so he pulled with all his might.

Hippo wasn't going to be beaten by Anansi, so he pulled with all his might.

"What has Anansi had for breakfast?" Elephant asked himself as he pulled. "He's as strong as Hippo."

"I don't believe it," said Hippo, as he pulled. "Anansi is as strong as Elephant."

The game of tug of war went on and on and on. Finally, when the sun was high in the sky, Elephant decided to give in. "It's no good. There's no way I can beat Anansi."

At the same moment Hippo decided to give in. "I will have to admit defeat," he said. "I cannot beat Anansi."

Anansi watched in delight as the rope fell to the ground. He ran to Elephant, who was sitting on the ground trying to catch his breath and looking exhausted.

"Do you admit I'm stronger than you?" Anansi asked.

"I don't know how," said Elephant, "but you are as strong as I am."

"So will you look where you are sitting next time?" asked Anansi.

"Yes, I will," said Elephant, reluctantly.

"Good. I'll collect my rope then," said Anansi.

Anansi quickly started to collect the rope and made his way to his favorite tree by the edge of the river. Here he found Hippo sitting on the ground, trying to catch his breath and looking exhausted.

"Do you admit I'm stronger than you?" asked Anansi.

"I would never have believed it," said Hippo, between deep breaths. "You are as strong as I am."

"I told you so," said Anansi, pleased he'd managed to trick both Elephant and Hippo on the same day.

• • •

Dear Reader

Thank you for buying and reading this book.

We hope you enjoyed this collection of Anansi The Trickster Spider stories. If you have, would you mind leaving a quick review on Amazon? As an indie publisher reviews help readers find us and our books.

Thank you from the Mad Moment Media team.

To find out about our other books please visit us at:
www.madmomentmedia.com

ABOUT THE AUTHOR

Lynne started writing professionally in 1997; mainly for UK-based magazines. Since that time, she has had over 25 books and more than 300 features published. Her books have been published in UK, USA, Canada, Holland, Australia, Korea and Indonesia. Her first picture book, *A Book For Bramble*, has been translated into five languages, whilst her second book, *The Best Jumper*, was recorded and aired on the BBC's CBeeBies radio channel.

To learn more about Lynne and her work visit:
www.lynnegarner.com

To find out more about Anansi and his friends, and to keep up to date with all their news please like our Facebook page.

www.facebook.com/madmomentmedia/

OTHER BOOKS AVAILABLE

Ten Tales of Brer Rabbit
Ten Tales of Coyote
Hedgehog of Moon Meadow Farm

BOOKS COMING SOON

Fox of Moon Meadow Farm

www.madmomentmedia.com

Printed in Great Britain
by Amazon

57905315R00066